GREAT BIG THINGS

By **Kate Hoefler**

Illustrated by **Noah Klocek**

HOUGHTON MIFFLIN HARCOURT
Boston New York

The world is full of great big things:

This enormous canyon.

This wide desert.

These billions of stars.

This single mouse who travels far

by an endless highway.

In the wind. This wind.

On a massive train, ten thousand tons,

with nothing but a single crumb.

Through a forest of a million trees.

By bears that amble there.

Past great big things you can't quite see,

with ever-climbing
bravery.

In a dark storm of a hundred clouds.

By a river's rushing falls.

To the ocean—vast and wide and deep,

with great big ways to drift to sleep.

By great big things: a sunset.

Sunrise.

Blue whales gliding, ninety feet.

In great big cold, great big sleet.

By towering sea cliffs.

Through frozen fields.

Up a mountain,

toward the moon

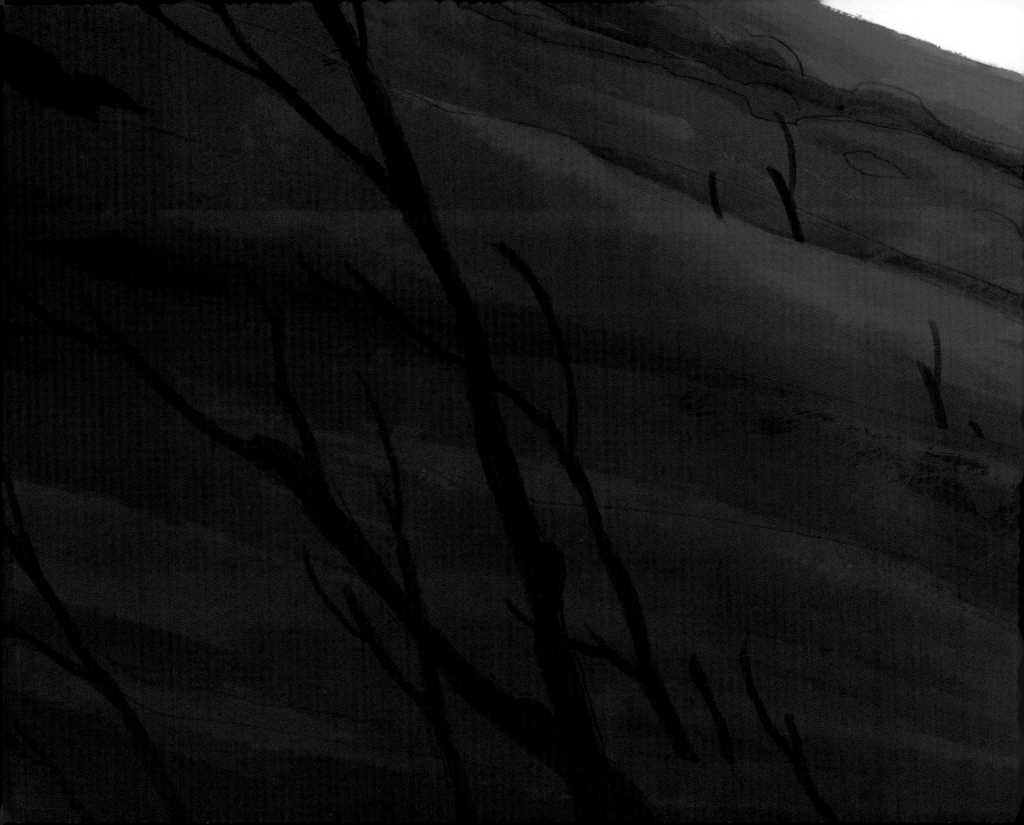

for a crumb:

It's a great big thing to love someone.

"But there were deserts and mountains,
a forest, the sea..."

"Small things."

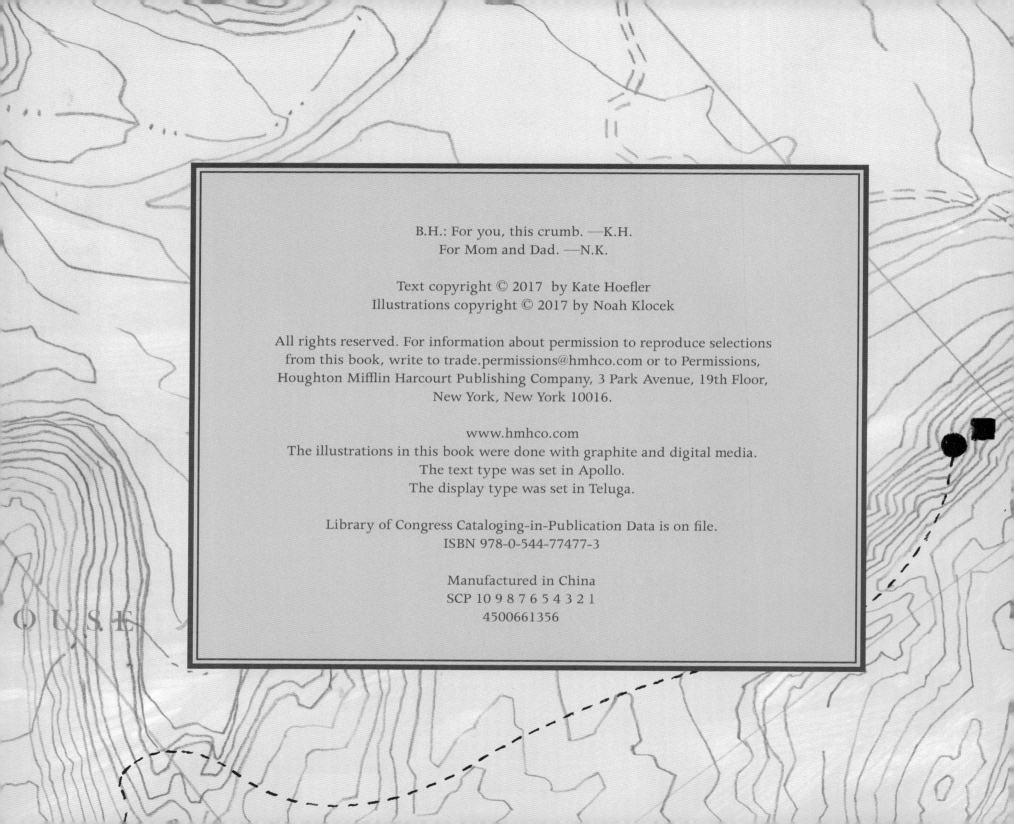

Text copyright © 2017 by Kate Hoefler
Illustrations copyright © 2017 by Noah Klocek

www.hmhco.com
The illustrations in this book were done with graphite and digital media.
The text type was set in Apollo.
The display type was set in Teluga.

Library of Congress Cataloging-in-Publication Data is on file.
ISBN 978-0-544-77477-3

Manufactured in China
SCP 10 9 8 7 6 5 4 3 2 1
4500661356